Alex Rance
TIGER'S ROAR
illustrated by Shane McG
ALLEN&UNWIN
SYDNEY • MELBOURNE • AUCKLAND • LONDON

Tiger was the champion of all the jungle.

He was strong, bold and proud,
and he sat at the top of the very tallest tree.

But one day the winds blew,

the birds shrieked,

the tree shook, and...

Tiger fell all the way down
to the mud at the bottom of the tree,
and bumped his head.

Tiger wobbled to his feet.
He tried to climb the tree again, but the branches he had used as a ladder were gone.

Again and again he tried, but it was no use. Tiger sat slumped in the mud. He tried a frustrated roar, but he couldn't even manage a little meow.

Just then, Howler Monkey came leaping out of the bushes.
He danced around muddy little Tiger,
hooting and pulling his tail.

But Tiger didn't say a word.

'What's the matter, Tiger?
Don't you want to play?'

Tiger shook his head.

'Have you lost your roar?' asked Howler Monkey.

Tiger nodded miserably.

'Don't give up! Why don't you howl like a monkey instead? That always works for me. I'm the loudest in the jungle.'

Tiger tried a howl, just a very little one,
then louder and louder

until he was howling
just like a monkey.

He was very pleased.

Hearing the strange loud howl,
Rabbit came to investigate.
'Hey hey, Tiger, it's you. I thought it was Howler Monkey.
What's up? Why are you all muddy?'

'I've fallen from the very top of my tree and I can't get back up,'
said Tiger, hanging his head.

'Why don't you try hopping? Hopping always works for me.
I can hop higher than anyone in the jungle. Hop, hop, hop!
Don't give up!' called Rabbit.

Tiger tried a hop,
just a very little one,

then higher and higher until
he had hopped all the way onto the first branch.
Tiger was delighted!

But when he tried to hop to the next branch, he hopped
too far and slid all the way back down into the mud.

Tiger lay at the bottom of his tree looking up at the high branches, wondering if he would ever make it back there again, when CRASH! Rhino appeared through the trees.

'Sorry, Tiger, I didn't see you there.
What are you doing down in the mud?' said Rhino.

'I've fallen all the way from the very top of my tree.
I've been howling and hopping but I still can't get back up.'

'Why don't you try being super strong?
That always works for me.
I'm the strongest in the whole jungle.
Don't argue. And don't give up!'

Tiger tried pushing over a tree,
just a very little one, and it worked!

He bounced around howling with excitement.

Tiger hopped onto the first branch of his tree, then used his new-found strength to push down another branch to use as a ramp. He pushed with all his might to build another, but the branch broke and Tiger fell all the way back down into the mud.

Meanwhile Silverback had been watching all the commotion. 'What are you trying to do?' Silverback asked, climbing down from his own tree.

'I've fallen from the top of my tree and I can't get back up. I've been howling like Howler Monkey, hopping like Rabbit and being strong like Rhino, but I'm still down here in the mud.'

'Why don't you stop and think. That always works for me. I'm the wisest in the whole jungle.'

Tiger tried to have a thought,
just a very little one,

but he was thirsty after all his hopping,

howling

and pushing.

So he went down to the river for a drink.

As he leaned over the water he saw his reflection
and was so surprised he nearly fell right in.
He saw Silverback's grey hair, and Rhino's horn, and Rabbit's hop,
and Monkey's howl, but he didn't see a proud tiger at all.

'I would prefer to be me at the bottom of the tree than something I'm not at the top,' he said.

Tiger tried a roar, just a very little one. Then a bit louder. Howler Monkey, Rabbit, Rhino and Silverback came dancing and hopping and charging in as fast as they could.

'Thank you for trying to help,' said Tiger.
'But these are YOUR talents.'

'Howler Monkey, your howl is what makes YOU special.'

'Rabbit, your hop is what makes YOU special.'

'Rhino, your strong horn is what makes YOU special.'

'Silverback, thank you for helping me be a bold proud tiger again, even though I am still at the bottom of the tree.'

All the animals looked up to the top of the very tallest tree in the jungle. It was a long way up.

'Do you think,' said Tiger, 'if we all use our own special talents and work as a team, we could climb the tree together?'

So Rhino pushed and pushed and built a sturdy mound of dirt halfway up the tree.

Then Rabbit hopped up into the higher branches to test which ones were strong enough to climb.

Howler Monkey shouted encouragement but he got so excited that he fell off his branch.

But just in the nick of time,
Tiger stuck out his tail for Monkey to grab.

'Tails never fail!' said the cheeky monkey as he swung back up.

Monkey howled.
Rabbit hopped.
At the bottom of the tree, Rhino grunted.
Silverback gave one final, helping push.
Tiger leaped...

...all the way up to the top of the tree.

Tiger had climbed from the mud to become the strong,
bold and proud champion of the jungle once again.

But he knew he never could
have done it without his loyal,
caring and very different friends.

You could hear Tiger's mighty roar
in every part of the jungle. 'It's good to be a tiger,
but it's even better to be a tiger with a team.'

First published by Allen & Unwin in 2018

Allen & Unwin
83 Alexander Street
Crows Nest NSW 2065
Australia
Phone: (61 2) 8425 0100
Email: info@allenandunwin.com
Web: www.allenandunwin.com

A catalogue record for this book is available from
the National Library of Australia
catalogue.nla.gov.au

ISBN 9 781 76052 391 6

For teaching resources, explore
www.allenandunwin.com/resources/for-teachers

Cover and text design by Sandra Nobes
Set in 24 pt LunchBox Bold by Sandra Nobes

This book was printed in July 2018 through The Australian Book Connection

3 5 7 9 10 8 6 4